Snoopy, Spike and the Cat Next Door

It's A "Sticky" Situation
When Spike Comes For A Visit

Based on the comic strip "Peanuts"
Created and Written by:
Charles M. Schulz

Produced and Directed by:
Lee Mendelson
Desirée Goyette

Original Music and Lyrics by:
Desirée Goyette

Music Arranged and Conducted by:
Ed Bogas

Art Director:
Frank Hill

"What Good Is A Cat?"

What good is a cat?
Just answer me that
Will he bring you your slippers and guard
   the house?
Or waste his time chasing a poor little mouse?
When you throw him a frisbee he won't bring
   it back
Knowing that–what good is a cat?

What good is a cat?
He eats and gets fat
He'll pretend to be loyal then give you the claw
He'll rip your upholstery then lick at his paws
He'll run off and leave at the drop of the hat
Think of that!–what good is a cat?

They think they're royalty
All because of some ancient Egyptian myth
But where's their loyalty?
One minute they're purring and…the next…
   they hiss!

What good is a cat?
They just leave me flat
They won't take a walk or a run in the park
If a burglar comes they won't even bark
They won't sit, they won't heel, they're too proud
   to do that
What good is a cat?

"Just Follow The Simple Directions"

Just follow the simple directions
A into B into C
Building can really be easy!
C into D into E
Just follow the simple directions
E into F into G, G into H into I
It's as easy as pie!

We have to be patient, we have to keep cool
There must be no short-cuts or tricks!
If we all work together
And follow the rules!
We'll get it done lickety-split!

Just follow the simple directions
I into J into K
Build it up section by section!
Hey, this could take us all day!
Now Lucy, no time for complaining!
L into M into N, N into O into P
Just think how great it will be!

Follow the simple directions
P into Q into R
Each piece has its own connection
We're doing okay so far!
Say, we're close to the finish!
R into S into T, T into U into V, WXY and Z!

THE
END